Black Beauty

Adapted by M.J. Carr
From the novel by Anna Sewell
Illustrated by John Speirs

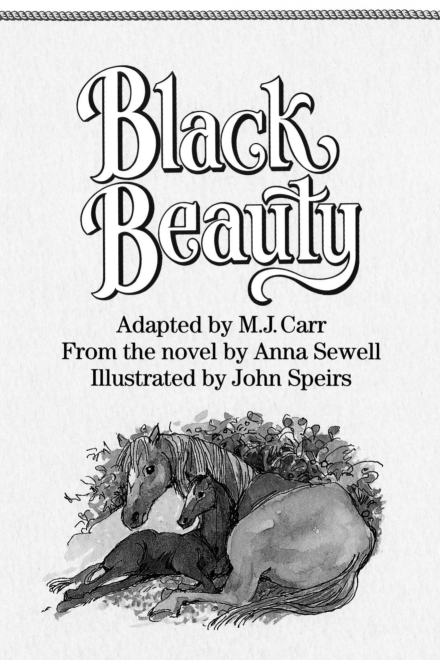

Scholastic Inc.
New York Toronto London Auckland Sydney

Book designed by David Tommasino

ISBN 0-590-48618-7

12 11 10 9 8 7 6 5 4 3 2 1   4 5 6 7 8 9/9

Printed in the U.S.A.   37

First Scholastic printing, August 1994

My Early Home

The first place that I can remember was a large pleasant meadow. As a colt, I lived there with my mother. The grass was sweet, and the air fragrant. I was born with a white star marking my forehead and one white foot. My coat was shiny and black.

The master who owned us was a kind man. Often, he came to the gate with carrots for my mother and pieces of bread for me. I galloped through the meadow with the other colts. Sometimes, we liked to play rough. My mother called me to her. "You must not bite or kick," she instructed me. "Or in any way be ill-bred. Always walk proudly and lift your feet up when you trot." I raced back to play with my friends, keeping in mind the advice my mother gave me. Each day I grew taller and more strong.

My Breaking In

When I was four years old, I overheard my master say that he must break me in. "Breaking in" is a very important time for a horse. It is when he is taught to wear a saddle and a bridle and to carry a rider. The first time my master put a bit in my mouth, I tried to yank free. A bit is a cold piece of hard steel that is pushed into a horse's mouth and held fast by straps. My master fit me with a saddle, which felt tight around my belly and heavy on my back. But he made it easier for me by offering me oats, which I loved. He stroked my neck and talked to me gently.

Soon I got used to the strange feel of the bit and the saddle. My master rode me around the meadow, then hitched me to a cart and taught me to trot steadily. When I had learned, he knew I was ready for sale.

"A horse never knows who will buy him," my mother told me. "I hope you fall into good hands. Some masters are thoughtful like ours. But others are foolish or cruel and ought never have a horse or dog to call their own. Still I say, do your best and keep up your good name."

I said good-bye to my mother. Later, I would have cause to remember what she said.

Birtwick Park

I was sold to a Squire who lived on an estate called
Birtwick Park. When I arrived, I was led to a large,
clean stall in a stable with other horses. It was airy and
pleasant. The coachman brushed my coat until it
shone like a rook's wing. He brought me to the Hall to
display me before Squire Gordon and his wife.

"What shall we call him?" the Squire asked.

"He really is quite a beauty," said his wife. "He has a sweet face and an intelligent eye. What do you say we call him Black Beauty?"

"Black Beauty," said Squire Gordon. "Yes. That will be his name."

Ginger

One of the other horses in the stable was a high-spirited chestnut mare named Ginger. Ginger was skittish, and known to bite. She and I were paired together to drive the Squire's carriage in a double harness. I wondered how we would get along.

Ginger proved to be a good partner. Our paces were much the same and I found it easy to keep step with her. But Ginger stayed nervous and alert. One day, when we were out grazing together, Ginger told me why.

"I didn't have an easy time as a colt, as you did," she said. "Before I came to Birtwick, I lived in a place where the grooms were rough. When it came time to break me in, they chased me down and wrenched my mouth open. When I reared and tried to get free, they flogged me. As time went on, they put the bearing rein on me."

"What's a bearing rein?" I asked.

"You've never worn one? It holds a horse's head up —for fashion, nothing more. I like to toss my head high, same as any proud horse. But the bearing rein strained all the muscles in my neck and made them ache. And the bit they used was sharp. It tore the corners of my mouth so I could barely eat my hay. The stalks bristled against my tender skin."

Our talk was cut short as our coachman came to groom me. The coachman's name was John Manly. He was not rough like the grooms Ginger described. When he took up the brush to work, he talked to me gently. John was careful of the tender places on my body, and the ticklish ones, too. He combed my mane until it was shiny and smooth. I couldn't help thinking, though, of the things that Ginger had described.

A Stormy Day

Soon after, the Squire had to travel to town on business. John hitched me to the dogcart, a light carriage with high wheels, and joined the Squire in the cart. That day, it had been raining quite heavily. The wind blew the leaves across the road in a shower. We drove until we reached a tollgate at a wooden bridge. The river was swollen, and was lapping at the bridge's rails.

"The river's rising fast!" said the man at the toll. I trotted across and on to town.

The Squire stayed at his business till late in the afternoon. By that time, the storm was raging. Winds howled. We set off on a road that took us through a dark wood. In some places, the road was flooded. The water reached halfway to my knees.

By the time we arrived at the bridge, it was dark. I was going at a good pace. But the moment my feet touched the planks, I knew that something was wrong. I made a dead stop.

"Go on, Beauty," said my master. He gave me a light touch with the whip to urge me on. When I would not go, he did so again.

John jumped out of the cart and tried to lead me forward. "What's the matter, Beauty?" he asked.

Just then the man at the tollgate ran out. "Hoy! Halloo! Stop!" he shouted. "The bridge is broken! The middle's been carried away!"

John took my bridle and turned me from the bridge. The river rushed cold and dark at our feet. "Good Beauty," he said. He knew that I had saved our lives.

As we traveled the long road home, I heard my master tell John that he thought animals were sometimes wiser than people. John told stories he'd heard about dogs and horses who'd helped people or saved them. When finally we reached home, I was rewarded with a supper of bran mash and crushed beans. John gave me an extra thick bed of straw that night. I was glad for it, for I was tired.

The Fire

Because ours was a large stable, John trained stable boys to help him. One day, a stable boy named James was entrusted to harness Ginger and me to the carriage and drive the Squire and his wife on a long journey.

We stopped overnight at an inn, and Ginger and I were stabled there by the hostler. A man came into the stable and lit his pipe, then climbed up to the loft to pull down some hay for his horse. I had often heard John say that no good could come of smoking a pipe in a stable, but I thought nothing of it, and drifted off to sleep.

I did not sleep through the night, though. When I awoke, I was choking and could not breathe. Smoke filled the stall. I heard a snapping, crackling sound. The stable was on fire!

Soon, all the horses in the stable were awake, pawing in their stalls, neighing and whinnying with fear. A hostler ran in and tried to lead me out of the burning stable, but I would not budge. The flames terrified me. I neighed frantically. I stamped and pulled at my halter.

Then James ran in. I recognized him through the thick smoke. When he reached me, he stroked my nose and talked to me to reassure me. He untied the scarf he wore around his neck and fastened it over my eyes so that I would not see the fire. He led me, blindfolded, out of the stall, then ran back in to save Ginger. When she was safe, we watched the flames torch up in a great blaze.

I was glad, afterward, to return to Birtwick, where the grooms loved the horses and were not careless.

Going for the Doctor

One night at Birtwick, as I was bedded down in the soft, clean straw of my stall, I was startled by the clanging of the stable bell. John ran in and harnessed me quickly, then mounted me and rode me to the door of the Hall. The Squire stood anxiously in the doorway. "Hurry, John!" he urged. "Get the doctor! The mistress is getting sicker!" John did not have to spur me on. I galloped as fast as my legs would travel to the doctor's house in town.

John leaped off me and pounded on the door. The doctor peered out the window. He was in his nightclothes.

"The mistress is sick!" John cried. "Come quickly!"

"My son took our only horse!" said the doctor.

"Take Beauty!" urged John. The doctor dressed, and mounted me in a flash.

Though I had galloped at quite a clip to get to town, and was quite winded, I galloped every bit as quickly back to the Hall. I delivered the doctor to the door. Then I was led to my stall by Joe Green, a young stable boy. I was still sweating and panting.

Joe was only fourteen and had not yet had much training. He did not know that he should put a blanket over my chilled body. He gave me a pail of water to drink, thinking I would be thirsty. But the water was cold and only chilled me more. By morning, I was sick, burning with fever. The farrier was called. He gave me a draught and waited to see how the medicine would take.

John hovered close to me, tending me with special care. "My poor Black Beauty," he said. "You saved your mistress's life." It was many days till I got well.

My mistress had not died that night, but she was no longer as strong as she had been. The doctor who attended her said she must move to a warmer place. The Squire began to make plans to sell his estate in order to move. John began to arrange for the sale of the horses. I wondered what would become of me.

Earlshall

One day, John rode Ginger and me some miles to a new home and bid us good-bye. I could not use words to say good-bye to my kind groom, so I nuzzled my nose in his hand. Our new home was an estate owned by an earl. It was known by the name Earlshall. The stables there were grand. Ginger and I were rubbed down and fed. We waited to see what would be required of us.

The first morning, Ginger and I were harnessed to the carriage and led to the front of the Hall. At the top of the steps stood the lady of the estate. She looked us over imperiously and sniffed.

"Why aren't their heads high?" she asked the coachman.

"They're not yet used to the bearing rein," he answered.

"Raise their heads at once!" she ordered. "They'll be used to it soon enough!"

The coachman put the bearing rein on us, which pulled our heads high, as Ginger had described. He did not fasten the rein tightly at first, wanting to accustom us to it by degrees. Still, I did not like the rein. I found it much harder to pull the cart. It was almost impossible to pull uphill, since horses go uphill by leading with their heads. Wearing the rein put a great strain on my back and my legs.

"Now you see what it's like," said Ginger. "If they fix the rein any tighter, I won't bear it!"

Each day, the coachman pulled the rein a notch higher. One day, the lady demanded that the reins be fixed to the highest notch, which made them quite painful. Ginger jerked nervously in the cart. The coachman approached her. He reached to tighten the strap of her rein, but Ginger reared up. She kicked and plunged desperately, knocking the coachman back. My mother had taught me to be well-bred with people, but she must not have meant people like these. I admired Ginger. She did not let the men hurt her.

Reuben Smith

One day our coachman went off to London and left another man, Reuben Smith, in charge of the stables. Reuben was a good man, but had a love of drink. One afternoon he rode me into town on an errand and stabled me there. He told the hostler he'd return soon. When he finally came to pick me up, though, it was past nightfall. I could tell that something was wrong. His voice was harsh and raspy and he smelled of drink.

The hostler had noticed that one of my shoes had come loose. He asked Reuben if he might fix it.

"It will be all right till we get home," Reuben replied gruffly.

The hostler urged Reuben to take care, but Reuben shook him off with an oath, then mounted me.

As soon as we were out of town, Reuben whipped me to a gallop. My shoe loosened more. I felt it fall off. The road we took was paved with jagged stones. As I galloped, one caught in my foot. I began to limp, but Reuben didn't notice. With each step I took, the rock cut deeper, splitting my hoof. Reuben only cursed, and whipped me to go faster.

Suddenly, my hoof split down to the quick. I could bear the pain no longer. My legs gave way beneath me and I fell violently upon my knees. Reuben toppled off and hit his head on the sharp stones. Then he did not move. I stood at the side of the road, waiting for someone to come along and find us. Nothing moved but the white clouds near the moon. My knees were broken and pained me greatly. I knew that I would never be the fine-stepping stallion I had once been.

"Look here!" It was some men from Earlshall. One raised up Reuben's head. There was no life. "He's dead!" he cried. "The horse has thrown him!"

"Well, no wonder," said the other, looking at my legs. "His knees are bad and his hoof's cut all to pieces!" They bound my foot in a handkerchief and led me slowly home.

My knees healed. But because they'd been broken,
they were now unsightly. The Earl no longer wanted
me in his stables. Once again, I was to be sold. The
groom came to get me one day when I was grazing
with Ginger in the pasture. He slipped a harness over
my head and led me off. I turned and neighed good-bye
to Ginger. She trotted along the hedge, neighing
anxiously back. She stood watching as I was led off
down the long road.

A Job Horse

This time, I'd been sold to a livery. There, I was a "job horse," pulling a carriage for anyone who rented me, a different driver each day. Some flopped the reins carelessly. Others cut me with the whip. The worst yanked me this way and that, driving the bit into the tender corners of my mouth. "Go along, you lazy beast!" they cried, though I did my best and worked hard every day. No one knew that I had once been an elegant stallion. No one knew my name was Black Beauty.

Soon, I was sold again. I hoped that my life would improve. But my new master knew little about horses. One of his grooms stole the oats from my stable and took them for his own use. The other let the straw rot in my stall and did not take care to clean my feet or to shoe me. Because of this, I developed a bad infection in my hooves and took a serious stumble. I was brought to the farrier, who said I had "thrush." He packed my feet with medicine, which was a very unpleasant business.

Over time, my hooves healed. But my master now thought horses too much trouble and no longer wanted me.

A Horse Fair

This time, I was sent to a horse fair, a market where horses are bought and sold. Many men came up to inspect me. They pulled my mouth open to look at my teeth, then felt my legs to judge my strength. I myself had become a good judge of men. I could tell by their voices which were kind and which were not. One man came to bid on me, a loud, harsh man. I hoped that he would not be my new master. Just as it seemed that he was going to buy me, another man arrived. This one was gentle. His eyes were kind. He bid more money than the first, and so became my master.

My new master's name was Jerry. He was a cab
driver in London. After he gave me a good feed of oats,
he rode me the long distance home. I had never been to
London before. There were streets to the right, and
streets to the left, streets crossing every which way.
When we reached the small house where Jerry lived, his
family spilled out the door. His wife was plump and
cheerful. His children pet me and laughed merrily.

"We'll call him Jack," said Jerry. And so I got a new
name, one more suited to a horse who pulled a cab.

A London Cab Horse

The work of being a cab driver's horse was often very hard. Each day Jerry harnessed me and took me out to work. We rushed travelers to their trains, and delivered those who were sick to their doctors. I didn't mind the work, though. Jerry and I understood each other as well as a horse and master can. Jerry never used a bearing rein and went easy on the bit, using the reins only lightly. He always left Sunday as a day of rest for us both.

One day, Jerry and I waited outside the park, in hopes of getting a passenger. Another cab pulled up next to ours. The horse who was drawing the cab was a chestnut. Her eyes were dull and weary. The bones of her neck showed through her skin. When I dropped a small mouthful of hay, she bent to pick it up. She lifted up her head and saw me.

"Black Beauty?" she asked. "Is that you?"

The old horse was Ginger! But so changed! As we waited by the park, Ginger told me all that had happened to her since last I'd seen her. She now worked for a large cab company. They made her work without rest every day of the week. The drivers often whipped her.

"You used to fight back when people mistreated you," I said.

"Ah," said Ginger. "I did once, but it's no use. People are stronger."

I put my nose up to hers to comfort her.

"You are my only friend," she said.

Just then, the driver of her cab came back and snapped her reins. I watched my old friend edge out into the London streets. I knew that she was too worn and feeble to be working so hard. Without rest, she would surely die. I knew that it was the last time I would ever see my old friend Ginger.

Jerry's New Year

Soon it was Christmastime. In London, Christmas is merry and bustling. Jerry and I worked hard and late. The week of Christmas, the weather was cold and damp. Jerry developed a cough. By New Year's, the weather was bitter. The rain had turned to sleet, and the wind whipped and whistled. Jerry and I dropped two men off at a party. They told us to return at eleven o'clock to pick them up and take them home.

We returned when we were told, but the lights of the party were still blazing. Jerry pulled our cab up to the curb and waited. He huddled in the cab for warmth. My own legs stiffened from the cold.

The men did not come out for hours, and when they did, they were drunk and loud. When we dropped them off, they grumbled about the fare. Jerry and I drove home in the chilly early hours of the new year. I noticed that Jerry had begun to cough harder. Both of us needed to get dry and warm, and take some rest.

The next morning was a workday. I woke up tired, but able. Jerry did not come out to harness me, though. I stayed in the stable, wondering where he was. Finally, his son and daughter came out to feed me. The little girl was crying. I could tell by what they said that Jerry had taken sick. The doctor had been sent for.

Days passed. I listened carefully to the talk in the stable. I learned that Jerry had bronchitis. His family feared he would die.

Slowly, Jerry began to mend, but the doctor was firm in his orders. Jerry's health was now fragile. The doctor told him he could no longer work as a cab driver, unprotected from the cold. He would have to take other work. I knew what this meant. Once again, I would be sold. The family bid me good-bye.

Hard Times

I shall never forget my next master. His voice was as harsh as the grinding of cart wheels over gravel stones. His name was Nicholas Skinner. Skinner was a cab owner who sent out many cabs. He was hard on the drivers and, in turn, the drivers were hard on the horses. My driver had a cruel whip with something sharp at the end. He whipped my belly and sometimes even my head.

One morning we waited at the railway station. A family with a good deal of luggage called for our cab. The little girl came over to pet me.

"Papa," she said. "This poor horse is weak and worn out. It is cruel to make him cart all our luggage."

"That's not my care!" snapped the father. He directed the porter to lift up the luggage. Box after box was lodged on the top of the cab. With a jerk of the rein and a slash of the whip, I was driven out of the station. I had had neither food nor rest for hours. The weight of the cab was great and exhausted me.

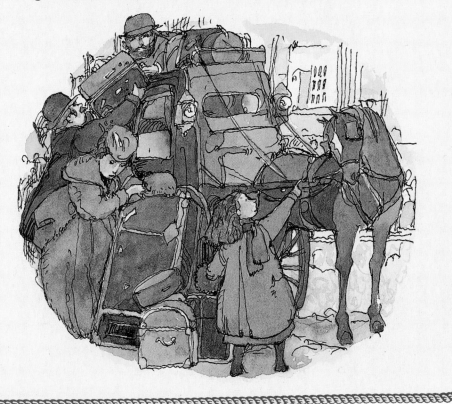

I got along fairly well until we came to a steep hill. I struggled to keep on, but my feet slipped out from under me. Suddenly, I fell heavily on my side and could not move. I thought it was the end, that I was about to die.

Someone loosened the throat strap of my bridle. I heard the policeman giving orders, but I couldn't open my eyes. After a time, with some coaxing, I revived enough to stagger to my feet. I was led back to my stables where Skinner and the farrier examined me. Skinner wanted to have me shot, but the farrier was kinder. He convinced Skinner to sell me. I wondered who would buy a horse so old and worn. My life was truly wretched. I had no strength or vigor left in my back or legs. I found myself wishing that I had died when I'd fallen.

Farmer Thoroughgood
and Willie

At the horse sale, fortune smiled on me. I was spotted by a kind man who had come with his grandson. The man had a broad, ruddy face and wore a wide-brimmed hat. I knew he must be a gentleman farmer.

"Here's a horse with fine breeding," he said, looking me over. "I think he has seen finer days."

"Please, can we buy him?" begged the boy.

The gentleman considered. "Perhaps if we feed him and let him rest, he will grow strong again. Then we might find him a good situation."

The gentleman's name was Mr. Thoroughgood. He bought me and took me home to his farm.

Under his care, I did indeed grow stronger. I was allowed to rest and was fed quite well. The grandson, Willie, even brought me carrots and pieces of bread. As I grew stronger, Mr. Thoroughgood began to inquire among his neighbors to find a place where I would be valued.

Down the road lived three genteel ladies. They required only light work, needing a horse to take them occasionally into town, nothing more. Mr. Thoroughgood went to visit the ladies and proposed that they buy me. The ladies were a little unsure.

"He has broken knees," one said. "That means that he's fallen. What if he falls again?"

Mr. Thoroughgood was confident in me. "Many first rate horses have had their knees broken through the carelessness of their drivers, and no fault of their own." He suggested that the ladies take me on trial, in order to see if they liked me. I hoped that these ladies would want to keep me. I had had too many masters. Now, I wanted a home.

My Last Home

The next morning, the ladies' groom came to pick me up. When we arrived at the stable, he took out his brush and began to clean my face. His touch was tender. I had not been groomed so gently in many a long day. The groom parted my forelock. He noticed the white star that marked me. Quickly, he looked at my legs. He saw the one white foot.

"Can it be?" he said. "Is it Black Beauty?"

I looked at the man. I did not recognize him.

"I'm Joe!" he said. "Joe Green, who used to care for you at Birtwick!"

Joe was the boy who had neglected to warm me the night I'd ridden to the doctor's. This man was grown, with a full chin of black whiskers. He was a skilled groom. But it was, indeed, my old friend!

Joe ran his hand tenderly over my knees. "I wonder who the rascal was who broke these," he said. He threw his arms around my neck, happy to see me after all these years. "I wish John Manly was here to see you, too! Beauty! Black Beauty!" he exclaimed. I nuzzled my nose against his.

Now, at my new home, the work is not hard. I pull the carriage for the ladies, who are pleased with my paces. Joe has grown into a fine, kind groom, and cares for me with great love. The ladies call me by my old name, Black Beauty. They've promised Joe that I'll never be sold.

And so, once again, I graze in a meadow, and think back on the happy days when I did so as a colt. The air is fragrant and the grass is sweet. I know, at last, I am home.